W9-CNH-369

The Sad Princess

Crabtree Publishing Company
www.crabtreebooks.com
1-800-387-7650

PMB 16A, 350 Fifth Ave.   616 Welland Ave.
Suite 3308,   St. Catharines, ON
New York, NY   L2M 5V6

Published by Crabtree Publishing in 2010

Series Editor: Jackie Hamley
Editor: Reagan Miller
Series Advisor: Dr. Hilary Minns
Series Designer: Peter Scoulding
Editorial Director: Kathy Middleton

Text © Lynne Benton 2007
Illustration © Andy Catling 2007

The rights of the author and the illustrator
of this Work have been asserted.

First published in 2007
by Franklin Watts
(A division of Hachette
Children's Books)

**Library and Archives Canada
Cataloguing in Publication**

Benton, Lynne
    The sad princess / Lynne Benton ; illustrated by
Andy Catling.

(Tadpoles)
ISBN 978-0-7787-3872-5 (bound).--
ISBN 978-0-7787-3903-6 (pbk.)

    1. Readers (Primary). 2. Readers--Princesses.
3. Readers--Sadness. I. Catling, Andy II. Title.
III. Series: Tadpoles (St. Catharines, Ont.)

PE1117.T33 2009h   428.6   C2009-903990-7

**Library of Congress
Cataloging-in-Publication Data**

Benton, Lynne.
    The sad princess / by Lynne Benton ; illustrated
by Andy Catling.
        p. cm. -- (Tadpoles)
    Summary: The princess is so sad that no one can
cheer her up, until two naughty monkeys come to
the palace.
    ISBN 978-0-7787-3903-6 (pbk.) -- ISBN
978-0-7787-3872-5 (reinforced library binding)
    [1. Princesses--Fiction. 2. Monkeys--Fiction.
3. Sadness--Fiction.] I. Catling, Andy, ill. II. Title.
III. Series.

PZ7.B44755Sad 2010
[E]--dc22

2009025300

The Sad Princess

by Lynne Benton

Illustrated by Andy Catling

Crabtree Publishing Company

www.crabtreebooks.com

Lynne Benton

"If you are feeling sad, like the Princess, then I hope this book will make you laugh!"

Andy Catling

"Being sad makes me mad which makes me sadder and so I get madder!"

The Princess was sad.

"A bag of gold to anyone who can make her laugh!" said the King.

A clown came.

But the Princess did
not laugh.

A magician came.

13

Still the Princess did not laugh.

A boy came with two monkeys.

They were very
naughty.

The King was not very happy.

But the Princess
laughed and laughed.

"Can I keep them?"
asked the Princess.

"Yes," said the boy.

"Oh no!" said the King.

Notes for adults

TADPOLES are structured to provide support for early readers. The stories may also be used by adults for sharing with young children.

Starting to read alone can be daunting. TADPOLES help by providing visual support and repeating high frequency words and phrases. These books will both develop confidence and encourage reading and rereading for pleasure.

If you are reading this book with a child, here are a few suggestions:

1. Make reading fun! Choose a time to read when you and the child are relaxed and have time to share the story.
2. Talk about the story before you start reading. Look at the cover and the blurb. What might the story be about? Why might the child like it?
3. Encourage the child to reread the story, and to retell the story in their own words, using the illustrations to remind them what has happened.
4. Discuss the story and see if the child can relate it to their own experiences, or perhaps compare it to another story they know.
5. Give praise! Children learn best in a positive environment.

If you enjoyed this book, why not try another TADPOLES story?

At the End of the Garden
9780778738503 RLB
9780778738817 PB

Bad Luck, Lucy!
9780778738510 RLB
9780778738824 PB

Ben and the Big Balloon
9780778738602 RLB
9780778738916 PB

Crabby Gabby
9780778738527 RLB
9780778738831 PB

Dad's Cake
9780778738657 RLB
9780778738961 PB

Dad's Van
9780778738664 RLB
9780778738978 PB

The Dinosaur Next Door
9780778738732 RLB
9780778739043 PB

Five Teddy Bears
9780778738534 RLB
9780778738848 PB

I'm Taller Than You!
9780778738541 RLB
9780778738855 PB

Leo's New Pet
9780778738558 RLB
9780778738862 PB

Little Troll
9780778738565 RLB
9780778738879 PB

Mop Top
9780778738572 RLB
9780778738886 PB

My Auntie Susan
9780778738589 RLB
9780778738893 PB

My Big, New Bed
9780778738596 RLB
9780778738909 PB

Night, Night
9780778738671 RLB
9780778738985 PB

Over the Moon!
9780778738688 RLB
9780778738992 PB

Pirate Pete
9780778738619 RLB
9780778738923 PB

Rooster's Alarm
9780778738749 RLB
9780778739050 PB

Runny Honey
9780778738626 RLB
9780778738930 PB

The Sad Princess
9780778738725 RLB
9780778739036 PB

Sammy's Secret
9780778738633 RLB
9780778738947 PB

Sam's Sunflower
9780778738640 RLB
9780778738954 PB

Tag!
9780778738695 RLB
9780778739005 PB

Ted's Party Bus
9780778738701 RLB
9780778739012 PB

Tortoise Races Home
9780778738718 RLB
9780778739029 PB